Secret Along the St. Mary's

Virginia B. Troeger
Illustrated by Michael-Che Swisher

SILVER MOON PRESS
NEW YORK

First Silver Moon Press Edition 2003
Copyright © 2003 by Virginia B. Troeger
Illustration copyright © 2003 by Michael-Che Swisher
Edited by Hope L. Killcoyne

The publisher would like to thank Lois Green Carr,
Historian at Historic St. Mary's City and the
Maryland Historical Trust, and Susan B. Zickel,
Interpretive Programs Coordinator, St. Mary's City, for fact checking.

For information:
Silver Moon Press
New York, NY
(800) 874–3320

Library of Congress Cataloging-in-Publication Data

Troeger, Virginia B.
    Secret Along the St. Mary's / Virginia Bergen Troeger ; illustrated by Michael-Che
Swisher.– 1st Silver Moon Press ed.
    p. cm. – (Mysteries in Time)
    Summary: In addition to having to cope with major changes in her family,
twelve-year-old Susannah, who lives in seventeenth-century Maryland, struggles with her
promise to keep the secret of a runaway indentured servant.
    ISBN 1-893110-35-4
    1. Maryland–History–Colonial period, ca. 1600-1755–Juvenile fiction. [1.
Maryland–History–Colonial period, ca. 1600-1775–Fiction. 2. Conduct of life–Fiction.
3. Indentured servants–Fiction.] I. Swisher, Michael-Che, ill. II. Title. III. Series.

PZ7.T7397Se2003
[Fic]–dc21

                                                                    2003050436

10 9 8 7 6 5 4 3 2 1
Printed in the USA

To my grandchildren – Trevor, Julia, Jasmine, Linnea, James, Keriann, Leah, and Martina.

—VBT

1

A VOICE IN THE WOODS
November 12, 1664

SUSANNAH CLARK STOOD IN HER DOORWAY. "Simon! Spark! Come! Race you to the river."

The shaggy, brown hounds who were dozing near the house jumped up and circled around her. Susannah straightened her dark braids under her cap, hiked up her apron and blue linen petticoat, and broke into a run. As always, Simon and Spark tore ahead and led the way down the well-worn path that cut through the dry autumn grasses to the shoreline. Though the first frost had passed, the November sun felt warm on her face.

When her mother had fallen sick with the dreaded fever a year ago, Susannah made wish after wish for Mama to get well often as she followed this short trail to St. Mary's River in southern Maryland. After a time Susannah came to call it the *wishing path.*

Now, months after Mama's death, Susannah still made wishes along the way, even though they didn't seem to come true. She wished that Papa's younger cousin Ellinore would soon arrive from England to help her with the housework. Since Papa would pay for Ellinore's ship passage, she would be his bonded servant for four years until she had paid her debt to him. He had received only one letter from her, but Susannah knew from Ellinore's warm words that she would be her friend.

Susannah also wished that William and Henry, her year-old twin brothers, could live at home. After Mama took sick, Papa arranged for the babies to stay across the river with the Hall family. The Halls lived on a large tobacco plantation owned by Mr. Samuel Laval, one of the richest farmers in the colony.

But most of all, again and again, Susannah wished that Mama were still alive.

Susannah sat quietly on the flat, sandy shore, sniffing the slightly salty tidewater, staring across her river, the St. Mary's River, which flowed on into the Potomac. Though not too wide, St. Mary's was deep enough for sailing ships to anchor. Susannah always hoped to spot a sailing ship from England anchored at Laval's landing. Seeing only the calm, gray water of late afternoon, she climbed into Papa's sturdy canoe to rest awhile. Her older brother Jonathan kept the canoe tied to a pine tree in a shallow cove where it was ready for passengers. Jonathan, serious and responsible, served as ferryman for travelers crossing

the river. Susannah knew that he rarely chatted in a casual way with his passengers. But he was a good and reliable ferryman, and received ample bags of tobacco as payment. Susannah fingered the dugout canoe, thinking of Jonathan's distant, close-mouthed ways, and how they displeased her. Yet, she pitied him, too. Not once since their mother's passing had she seen a smile pass his lips. He seemed far older than his fifteen years.

Susannah lifted her gaze to the waterfront, as always, watchful for settlers and traders passing by with news and greetings. In summer she often pulled off her shoes and black stockings to wade in the cool, lapping water. But never could she linger for long.

Even by late afternoon, Susannah's work wasn't finished. As housekeeper for her family she still had many chores to do before bedtime. She had to milk Brown Betty the cow, set out supper, clean up afterward, sweep the hearth, and fix the fire for the night.

Simon and Spark splashed nearby, fetching the sticks Susannah tossed to them. It was pleasant and soothing—as carefree as her life got—but all too soon she noticed the afternoon shadows growing longer. She jumped from the canoe to gather the last sprigs of purslane not caught by the frost. They would be good sallet greens for supper.

When she turned to head toward home, Susannah

noticed the dogs had disappeared into the dark pines. The tall trees separated the Clarks' fields from Asa Orrick the Elder's fields farther downriver. Susannah called and clapped her hands, but the barking hounds paid no heed.

Puzzled, she followed them into the woods. Simon and Spark were usually ready to lead the way home. As the shadows surrounded her, Susannah was startled by a distant voice shouting, "Call off your dogs!"

2

A PROMISE

PEERING DEEPER INTO THE WOODS, SHE SPOT-
ted a tall, slender young man. As she came closer
she noticed a bulky cloth bag slung on his shoulder.

"Stay still," called Susannah. "The dogs won't
hurt you."

When she saw the young man up close, she said,
"You're a servant of Mr. Orrick's, aren't you?
Benjamin Duckett. Where are you headed this late
in the day?"

Susannah patted Simon and Spark, who finally
stopped circling Benjamin and came to her side.
Benjamin clumsily shifted his bag to his other
shoulder. He yanked off his knit cap and combed his
fingers through his sandy hair. His ears, bright pink,
were quite large, a comic contrast to the serious
look on his face.

"I'm . . . I'm carrying a message from my master
to Samuel Laval across the river."

"Now? Darkness is fast falling!" She scanned his face. Something about the sadness of his eyes conjured up a hazy memory of him, but she couldn't recall what it was.

He looked about him. "Yes, 'tis late. I should turn back. I thought Mr. Orrick's log canoe was tied up at the water. I had forgotten that his son, Asa the Younger, took it. Some time ago, he took it, I think. He went upriver to oversee their faraway fields. So I . . . I started to walk. Maybe catch a lift across the water."

Susannah stared at Benjamin's pale face and his clenched fists. He seemed nervous and confused. Suddenly she remembered where she had last seen him.

"You came to Mama's funeral last spring," she said softly. "I remember how kindly you spoke to my father and me."

"Ay, I felt bad for you," Benjamin said, twisting his cap in his hands. "You looked so alone. And with those tiny babies to tend."

"I'm still lonely," Susannah said with a sigh. "Papa and my brother Jonathan are lonely, too. We had to send the twins away to be cared for across the river."

"They're with Goodman and Goodwife Hall at Laval's plantation, aren't they?"

"Why, yes," replied Susannah, "but how did you know?"

7

"I delivered some tools to Goodman Hall one day. I saw the twins and inquired after you and your father."

Susannah felt her face redden when she realized that Benjamin had especially asked about her. She also noticed that he kept edging away toward the riverbank and yet kept talking to her. His brown eyes darted nervously. He couldn't seem to stand still.

"My own mother died two years ago," Benjamin continued. "After that, my father put me on a ship in Liverpool bound for this wretched place. His farm was failing and there wasn't a job for me. Mr. Orrick the Elder paid my ship passage. I must work for him for six years before I'm a freedman. And to think my father said I'd make my fortune here. What folly!"

"Why do you have to work for six years?" asked Susannah. "Folks serve only four years here."

"I'm only fifteen. I can't get freedom dues till I'm twenty-one. It's six long years till I'm on my own and can buy land for a farm."

Susannah heard the bitterness in his voice. She saw the fear mixed with sadness on his face.

"My brother Jonathan's fifteen. He can't wait till he's sixteen and can serve in the militia, like Papa does. I want to be older too, I guess." Susannah quickly wondered why she'd said this. Girls and women were scarce in Maryland and usually were married by fifteen or sixteen. She used to tell Mama that she wasn't sure she wanted to marry and have babies. But Mama always laughed and said Papa would help her choose a good, honest planter for a husband.

"How old are you, then?" asked Benjamin.

"Thirteen come January."

He nodded and looked down, then back over his shoulder. With the heavy force of Simon or Spark jumping up against her chest, Susannah suddenly realized what was wrong.

"You're running away, aren't you?" she whispered and quickly covered her mouth with her hand as the words flew out.

"No, no, I wouldn't do that. It's wrong. I already told you. I'm taking a message to Mr. Laval from my master." Benjamin turned as if to run away right then but stopped short and stared at Susannah. "How, how did you know?" he stammered, his hands trembling.

"It's too dark to take out a boat now or wave down a ride," said Susannah. "Jonathan never crosses the river at night unless there's a full moon. There's only a first quarter moon tonight." She pointed to the grainy, gray sliver in the darkening sky.

Benjamin straightened his shoulders as if to gain strength.

"Mr. Orrick the Elder is sick," said Benjamin. "He can't take care of his tobacco plantation. His son is

upriver, too far away. He has his own plantation to attend to. So Jacob Hewett, one of the hired men, oversees the servants and the land."

"Yes, Papa told me old Mr. Orrick is doing poorly."

"Jacob Hewett was to teach me the cooper's trade, but he won't. He tells me I'm not strong enough to make barrels. I work all the time at the hoe. He whips me and has turned the other servants against me."

"He cannot do that!" exclaimed Susannah. "You must report him to Tobias Pierce, Mr. Orrick's other hired man. Papa speaks well of Tobias."

"But Jacob Hewett will find out and punish me more," stammered Benjamin. "It's hard when you're not your own master."

"You have rights," answered Susannah. "Papa goes to the justices at county court in St. Mary's City when something bad happens. He sat on a jury, too."

"Your family's free, Susannah. Old Mr. Orrick owns me. I can't go to court."

"Papa says anyone who's not treated fairly can go to the justices."

"There's something else." Benjamin lowered his voice to a whisper. "Jacob Hewett accuses me of trying to steal Mr. Orrick's finest fowling piece."

"Did you?" asked Susannah.

"No, no! It hangs over Mr. Orrick's fireplace in his plantation house. Yesterday his door was open.

I went inside and lifted it down. It's such a big gun, I just wanted to know how heavy it was, how it would feel to carry such a piece over my shoulder. But Jacob Hewett came by before I could hang it up again. He called me a common thief and said he would have the sheriff lock me in jail."

Susannah shook her head. She didn't know what to say. She didn't know how to help Benjamin. He seemed so alone and miserable.

"I must hasten on my way," Benjamin went on. He stuck his cap back on, lopsided, so that one ear stuck out. Susannah's heart went out to him.

"Where will you go?" she asked.

"I'll head upriver. Maybe to the Indians' village. I'm told they let settlers stay with them sometimes and work." Benjamin stopped and stared at Susannah. "I've spoken too much. Will you promise me, please promise me, that you won't tell anyone about seeing me? Not even your father. I'll take my chances anywhere to be away from Jacob Hewett. Somehow, someday, I'll pay back Mr. Orrick. I'll make things right. I will."

Susannah's mind began filling with fears for Benjamin. What would he eat? What would happen to him if he were caught? Maybe not telling anyone that he was running away wasn't wise. She needed time to think. But the look on his face and the feeling in her heart wouldn't let her wait.

"I'll keep your secret, Benjamin," she heard her-self say. "I promise. God speed." She started to reach out and touch his arm, but he had already disappeared into the silent pine trees. Simon and Spark looked up to her trustingly.

As Susannah stood in the gathering darkness, her fears for Benjamin took shape. What would he do for food? It was too cold now to pick berries. Where would he sleep? If Benjamin were caught, his master might severely beat him at a whipping post, and he would surely have more time added onto his term of indentured servitude. She felt hot tears when she thought of the whippings. But she knew she must linger no longer. She was long late for milking.

3

MANY WORRIES

STILL CLUTCHING HER SALLET GREENS, Susannah tore back up the wishing path, the dogs at her heels. When she spotted Brown Betty near the cow pen, she knew just how late she was. Jonathan must have brought their half-wild cow in for milking. And there was Papa waiting at the door, hands on his hips.

Papa was, as Mama used to say, "neither tall nor short." His red hair was thinning, his face lined and weather-beaten, but his blue eyes never wavered in their gaze.

"Susannah, where have you been? You've left the fire too long. Jonathan used much kindling to raise the flame."

"I'm sorry, Papa. It won't happen again." As she stepped inside the house, she smelled the smoke curling from the new logs. The blaze should have turned to red embers by now.

"I should say not. What were you doing? We thought something had befallen you at the water. I was just leaving to search for you."

"No, no. I'm not hurt. I followed the dogs into the pines. I thought they were chasing a fox. I ran too far and . . . and lost my way."

"That's not like you, Susannah. You know these woods well."

"It was getting dark, Papa. I couldn't see." She grabbed the broom by the hearth and lowered her eyes as she swept away the ashes.

Papa looked closely at her and took a deep breath. "We will speak of it no more. Put down the broom, eat your corn porridge, and prepare the house for the night." He turned away and filled his pipe from the rope of tobacco tied at his waist.

Susannah wished he had shouted at her and showed his anger, but Papa always kept his feelings hidden away. If only he had asked more questions. She was certain she would have blurted out the truth about Benjamin.

Too unsettled to eat the porridge, Susannah cleared the table and swept the hearth again. She was glad that the three of them—Papa, Jonathan, and Papa's servant, Marmaduke Gates—were outside. They always smoked their clay pipes and talked awhile after supper. She heard their voices and knew they were leaning on the chicken coop beyond the kitchen garden.

Susannah pictured Jonathan and Marmaduke together. Her brother was long and lanky with a heavy mane of red hair. A head shorter, Marmaduke was stocky, good-natured, and full of talk. He was twenty-two and would be a freedman in a few months. After that he would marry Mary Catherine Sheppy, who worked at the Orrick plantation. If anyone could coax conversation out of Jonathan, it was Marmaduke.

She looked up, startled to see Jonathan looming in the doorway. "Susannah, I had to catch Brown Betty tonight and milk her. Milking is not a man's work." He crossed his long arms across his chest.

"I know, Jonathan," murmured Susannah with a sigh.

"You'll have to wait awhile to bank the fire for the night. Don't fall asleep before you fix it."

Before Susannah could answer him, Jonathan disappeared out the door again. She wearily turned to get ready for bed. She untied her apron and the small drawstring bag she used as a pocket. After pulling off her bodice and stepping out of her petticoat, she hung them on a peg on the side wall. She kept on her white linen shift. This she wore as a nightgown.

Susannah and her father slept on feather mattresses in the main room of their small, clapboard

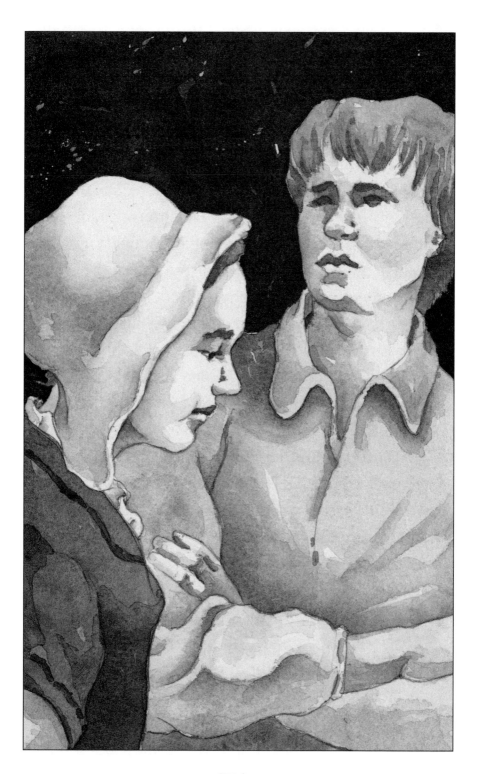

house. The settlers called this room the hall. Jonathan and Marmaduke climbed a ladder to sleep in the loft overhead. One of the dogs usually spent the night near the hearth, while the other stayed outside to scare away the wolves from the chicken coop.

Finally, after banking the fire, Susannah knelt down on her mattress to say her prayers. She prayed that God would keep her family healthy and safe. She wanted to pray for Benjamin, but how could she pray for someone who was breaking the law of the land? She wondered also if she should pray at all after making such a foolish promise and not telling her father the truth about why she was late.

Tired as she was, her jumbled thoughts kept her tossing and turning. Had she told Papa the truth, he would have sent word to the nearby farmers and the sheriff, who would have organized a search party. Benjamin would not get far before he was brought back to be punished. And he would know that she had broken her promise to him. Perhaps Mama would have understood how mixed-up everything had become in such a short time. She would have understood the gray, shadowy parts between things that were right and things that were wrong. Susannah thought of the time when she had let the dogs in at dinnertime one cold afternoon. Spark and Simon had leaped onto the table and started gobbling up a roast duck. Papa was furious, but Mama smiled and quietly shooed the dogs outside, ladling up extra corn pudding for everyone.

As Susannah listened to the wind whistling between the boards of their house, another frightening thought came to her. She was breaking the law herself by not reporting a runaway servant. With her heart thudding loudly, she wanted only to forget everything and sleep. But she could not erase Benjamin's sad face from her mind. She pulled her mattress close to Spark's warm body and finally fell into a troubled, dreamless slumber.

4

A SERIOUS LOSS

EVERYONE WOKE WITH THE FIRST LIGHT OF morning to begin work. Susannah shivered as she dressed in the previous day's clothes. She stirred the fire and added new logs to the dying embers. She swung the iron pot hook holding the kettle of food closer to the fire. There would be warm corn porridge for breakfast.

Susannah decided to coax Brown Betty into her pen now and milk her later. Wrapping herself in a woolen shawl against the early morning chill, she went outside.

As she chased the cow toward the pen, Susannah glanced toward the river and stopped short. Where was their canoe?

Forgetting Brown Betty, she flew down the path to the water. As far as she could see, the shore line was empty. All she found was the rope, one end still tied to the pine tree. The untethered end floated in the water.

Susannah turned back, but her feet slowed when she thought of Jonathan. He would surely think she had loosened the rope yesterday and let the canoe drift away. Then with a jolt she remembered Benjamin. Could he have taken the canoe last night to make his escape? No, no, he didn't take it. Benjamin wasn't a thief. She was certain of that. Or was she? He was sad and kind and too fearful to seek help. But where was their boat, if he hadn't stolen it? Their canoe had always been safe at the waterfront.

Susannah took a deep breath and walked back inside the house to break the news to Papa, Jonathan, and Marmaduke. "Our boat's gone! It was there when I came from the river last evening! Just the rope is there!" As she spoke, her stomach lurched, and she felt the blood rush to her face.

The men stared at her from their places at the table. Jonathan was the first to speak. "How can I ferry travelers across the river? Were you in that boat yesterday, Susannah? Is that why you were so late? You must have loosened the rope and forgotten to knot it tightly to the tree before you came home."

"I sat in it for a short spell," Susannah admitted. "But I didn't touch the rope."

"Susannah, you know better than to get in the canoe without Papa or me," said Jonathan, his tone winter-cold.

"I know you couldn't ferry travelers without it,"

said Susannah, her voice rising. "The boat's important to me too, Jonathan. We couldn't visit the twins on Sundays. I wouldn't set it adrift."

"You were the last one to see it," Jonathan went on. "What about the dogs? Did you see one of them chewing on the rope?" Abruptly he pushed away from the table and kicked open the door.

"Susannah, Jonathan, silence," said Papa, raising his hand. "Marmaduke, before you start work this morning in the tobacco house, hike along the riverbank as far as the Orricks' place. Maybe the rope gave way, and the canoe drifted farther downriver in the night wind. I heard a swift gale blowing last night."

"Shall I go now?" asked Marmaduke, standing up and grabbing his woolen hat from the wall.

"No," said Papa "Take your leave after you've finished eating. And Marmaduke, call out to anyone passing on the river that our canoe is lost. God willing, we'll find it soon."

Susannah told herself she wouldn't follow the wishing path that afternoon. She didn't want to see the empty canoe rope again. But when Simon and Spark came around near sunset, she gave in and headed for the water.

"Of course, my first wish today will be to find our boat," she told the dogs. "And my second wish too. Then I'll wish for Cousin Ellinore to come, for the twins to come home, and for Mama to be here. Then

I'll wish for a way to let go of Benjamin's secret. Then one more wish for the boat."

Susannah felt uneasy at the river and decided not to stay long. After scanning the empty waterfront once again, she quickly gathered an apronful of kindling wood and returned home.

As Susannah stirred the savory supper stew of beans and bacon flavored with thyme and sage, Jonathan burst into the house.

"Papa, Papa!" he called breathlessly.

"Yes, Son, I'm here at the table. What troubles you?" He looked up from the knives he had been cleaning.

"Jacob Hewett's coming across the fallow fields. He says he has important news."

"Mr. Orrick's plantation overseer must have something to fume about," said Papa with a small smile. "He's not a man who brings good tidings. Show him in, Jonathan."

Jacob Hewett's huge square-shouldered frame shadowed the doorway. His dark, bearded face glared at them. His bellowing voice filled the room. "Goodman Clark, that thief Benjamin Duckett ran away last night from Asa Orrick's plantation. By now he's probably with the Indians or following the creeks to the broad waters. If he comes sneaking around here, tie him up with a stout rope and summon me forthwith. He must be severely whipped

and will have to work many more days to serve out his indenture."

Before anyone could say a word, Jacob abruptly turned to leave.

"Hewett," called Papa, "stay awhile. We've not finished speaking. Susannah, fetch that barrel in the corner for Goodman Hewett to sit upon."

Susannah pushed an overturned barrel toward Jacob Hewett. He straddled it clumsily and sat down with a groan.

"Why do you call Benjamin Duckett a thief?" asked Papa. "Has he stolen something from Mr. Orrick?"

"That worthless boy has stolen your canoe, Matthew Clark," roared Jacob with a sneer. "Early this morn your servant told me himself that your boat's gone, didn't he? And two days ago Benjamin Duckett tried to steal Asa the Elder's finest fowling piece. I caught him with it in his hands while he was trespassing in the Orricks' house. Ha!"

Susannah's heart pounded as she thought of Benjamin. She kept her eyes lowered and hoped no one would question her.

"How can we be so sure that he stole our canoe?" said Papa. "He may be innocent."

"That lazy oaf took your boat to escape from his work," said Jacob, "serious crimes both." He stood up and squinted his hawkish black eyes at Susannah.

"Be on the watch for him. Even you, lass!"

Susannah felt her stomach turn over as Jacob went on talking. "I have extra work to do tonight because of that runaway and must be off." He rose stiffly and tramped out the door.

The three men sat in the tense silence. Finally, Marmaduke spoke up. "I talked with Benjamin one day. He was frightened and lonely. Said Hewett didn't always give him enough to eat."

"Yes," said Papa, "I heard old Asa's other servants complain about Jacob Hewett last year. He is a hard and often cruel taskmaster."

"Our boat is gone, and Benjamin Duckett escaped at the same time," said Jonathan pointedly to Marmaduke. "It had always been safe at the river."

"Jonathan," said Susannah with more strength in her voice than she felt. "Your boat pole wasn't in the canoe. Benjamin wouldn't have been able to move it."

"Susannah," said Jonathan, "he wouldn't need our pole. He could easily cut down a strong branch. A thieving servant like Benjamin wouldn't run away without an axe and a knife. Our canoe has gone for good. There's no question about that."

Susannah had to restrain herself from telling Jonathan that she could well attest to Benjamin's lack of an axe. She looked at him, her lips pressed together. He gave her a curious look.

"We must trust God to help us," said Papa. "Come spring, we'll barter with the Indians for another log canoe. Now let us sit down for our evening blessing and supper."

Susannah bowed her head but didn't close her eyes. She watched Papa as he prayed for Mama's soul and for the health of all the settlers. How tired and worn he looked. First Mama dying, then the babies going away, and now this trouble about the boat.

After their stew and cornbread, Susannah set out a bowl of yellow apples for dessert.

"This year's apples have been the best we've ever had," said Papa. "At last our apple orchard is growing well. How my good wife would have enjoyed them."

"Yes," said Susannah. "Mama liked to smell the blossoms in the spring too." Susannah felt warm tears flood her eyes. She turned toward the hearth so Papa wouldn't notice. Everyone stopped talking for what seemed to her a long time. Finally Marmaduke got up to light his clay pipe from a hot coal on the hearth, a kind smile on his boxy face. "Your stew was mighty tasty tonight, Susannah. Beans and bacon are my favorite."

"Everyone ate it up, didn't they?" said Susannah more cheerfully.

"Expect you'll be glad when Ellinore comes," he continued. "You've had much heaped on your shoulders this past year."

"My daughter has worked hard to keep house for us. I'm proud of her," agreed Papa.

Susannah smiled at her father and Marmaduke and even Jonathan, but it was a smile tinged with sadness and guilt. Papa would certainly not be proud if he knew she was keeping Benjamin's secret. A secret that was already beginning to unravel.

5

ELLINORE

SEVERAL MORNINGS LATER SUSANNAH GLANCED toward the river as she scattered grain to the squabbling hens and rooster. With a start she stopped and stared. There it was, the long-awaited ship from England sailing toward Laval's Landing! It was a middling-sized tall-masted vessel painted red, blue, and yellow.

The ship would be bringing seeds, dishes, buttons, sewing thread, linen, cotton, wool, and other goods for the colonists. A few passengers might be on board. In the spring the vessel would return to England loaded up with the settlers' barrels of tobacco to be sold in Europe.

Susannah flew back inside the house, calling, "The ship's in! Come, look!"

Papa, Jonathan, and Marmaduke hurried outside from breakfast.

"She's coming in at a good pace," said Papa.

"And she looks in fair shape after the crossing," said Marmaduke.

Jonathan, arms crossed, said nothing.

"Maybe Cousin Ellinore will be aboard?" asked Susannah.

"God willing," answered Papa. "She's due to arrive at any time now."

"How will we meet Cousin Ellinore with no boat?" asked Jonathan sourly.

"Don't worry," said Papa. "Mr. Laval knows our boat's gone. One of his servants will ferry her over."

"We should be there to meet her ourselves," mumbled Jonathan. "She's had a long voyage."

"I feel certain that Ellinore will understand," replied Papa patiently. "And now, Jonathan, I want you to mend the fences around the cornfield. Start at the south end."

"Yes, Papa," answered Jonathan without looking up.

"I must hasten to ready the house should Ellinore be on the ship," said Susannah. "I wonder what she'll bring with her."

"A few clothes and a bedroll," said Papa. "All her garments will need a good washing."

When the menfolk left, Susannah milked Brown Betty. She carried the tub of milk to the spring to keep it cool. She put sweet potatoes in the hot coals to roast for noon dinner and reminded herself to grind extra corn for Ellinore. "And I must find a spoon and bowl for her also," Susannah said out loud. She smiled at the sweet memory of Mama, who had often talked to herself, too.

Near noon Susannah heard strange voices outside. They didn't sound like Papa and Marmaduke coming in for noon dinner. She ran to the door to see a young woman of about seventeen striding up the path. She was wearing a wrinkled dark dress and tattered gray shawl. Strands of light, windblown hair had slipped from her cap and curled around her pale, friendly face. A young man balancing a battered chest on his shoulder followed her. Susannah recognized him as Samuel Laval's servant Lewis.

"You must be Cousin Ellinore!" called Susannah, running to her. "I've watched and watched for your ship to come in!"

"Yes, I'm Ellinore Paddington. And you're Cousin Matthew's daughter!" Susannah and Ellinore smiled, held hands, and finally put their arms about each other.

"Call me Susannah. Papa couldn't meet you because our canoe's gone."

"I've heard about your boat. A man called Samuel Laval and his servant met the ship and came aboard as soon as we dropped anchor. He told me about your lost boat. Lewis rowed me across the river."

Ellinore turned to Lewis. "Thank you kindly. You

can leave my chest outside the door. My clothes are filthy and filled with lice and, I fear, cockroaches."

"I'll report to Mr. Laval that you're safely here," said Lewis. "Good fortune to you in Maryland." He waved and strode off toward the river.

"I'm glad to be starting a new life, even though I'll be a bonded servant to Cousin Matthew for four years," said Ellinore. "And I'm glad to feel solid ground under my feet after those long, long days and dark nights rocking on the ship."

"Come inside," said Susannah. "You must be very, very tired. I'll fix you a wet cloth to wash your face and hands."

Ellinore nodded and followed Susannah into the house.

"Were you seasick?" asked Susannah, as she turned the potatoes on the coals.

"Oh my, yes! I had some very bad times. At first I was so weak I couldn't get up off my mat. Our sleeping quarters were hot, cramped, and smelled bad. Finally the sea calmed, and I could breathe fresh air on the deck. I felt better but didn't dare eat much, not that there was much fit to eat anyway!"

"What did you have?"

Ellinore laughed. "Hard, moldy biscuits, stew with tough, stringy pieces of salted meat, and precious little water."

"You won't be hungry here," said Susannah. "We

eat fresh fish, clams, oysters, squirrel, rabbit, turkey, smoked pork, and fruits and vegetables, except in the dead of winter, when it's mostly corn, corn, corn. We had a big kitchen garden when Mama was alive, but weeds have sprung up everywhere now. We do have sweet potatoes and a few herbs that came up by themselves."

"Come spring I'll help you plant vegetables," said Ellinore. "Do you have seeds?"

"Oh, yes," said Susannah, "we've saved some and we can buy more at Laval's store across the river. Mr. Laval sells many things in a room off his house." She paused and looked warmly at Ellinore. "I'm so glad you're here. You look just the way I thought you would, with blue eyes like Papa's."

"I'm glad to be here, Susannah. I'm sure I'll work hard to pay off my debt to your father, but I don't mind. I'm just happy to be in a place where people don't have to pay a fine if they don't go to the king's church."

"Is that why you wanted to come?" said Susannah.

"Not really," said Ellinore. "We lived near the seacoast, and ever since I was small I wanted to know what was on the other side of the great ocean." Ellinore lowered her voice. "Can you keep a secret, Susannah?"

"Yes, I can," agreed Susannah immediately.

Benjamin and his secret popped into her head. She quickly chased him out of her thoughts.

"My mother wanted me to marry a dull young lad who lived near us," explained Ellinore. "He plies no trade and owns no land. He doesn't have much future. When your father's letter came asking me to come to Maryland, I wanted to sail away as soon as I could find a ship to take me."

Susannah gazed at Ellinore in amazement. How different she was from Benjamin. She was happy to be here, even though she had four long years of work ahead of her. Benjamin seemed to hate being owned by someone else. But then, he was badly treated. Ellinore was already one of the family.

Susannah showed Ellinore about the hall and their small kitchen behind the fireplace. She pointed out the salt box, the many ears of corn hanging from the rafters, the big barrel of Indian corn kernels, the wooden mortar, and the long iron pestle used for grinding the daily corn into cornmeal.

"Pounding corn every day is the longest and worst job of all," said Susannah. "It seems to take till doomsday to turn the kernels of corn into cornmeal. Right now, the kernels aren't too tough, but they dry out during the winter and get harder and harder to pound. I'm tired of the dusty smell of the cornmeal, too. Papa wants to get a small grinding mill some-day. I hope it will make the grinding easier."

"At least you now have two more hands to help you," said Ellinore, holding up her hands and spreading her fingers apart. "But you'll have to show me what to do. I've never seen corn before."

"Well, first you have to cut the kernels off the cobs, soak them for a while to soften them, and drop them in the mortar," explained Susannah. "Then you take the pestle and pound and pound and pound and when the meal is all ground, you sift it through a sieve to separate the grains from the bigger pieces."

"And finally bake the meal into cornbread?" asked Ellinore.

"Yes, the sifted grains go into cornbread, but the larger bits and pieces have to be soaked overnight. Then," Susannah continued with a huff of weary good humor, "you have to boil them for hours on end. Once that's done you can make cornmeal mush, corn pudding, and corn cakes. In summer we roast fresh ears for corn on the cob and add fresh kernels in our deer, duck, chicken, and fish stews." Susannah crossed her arms. "Now you know all there is to know about corn."

Ellinore nodded, smiling. They strolled outside to inspect the chicken coop and the cow pen where Brown Betty was milked.

"Maryland farmers don't fence in their cows and hogs," Susannah explained as they headed for the freshwater spring. "They run free to find their own food. It costs less than fencing them in and having to feed them. That's why planters cut notches or marks in their animals' ears, so they can tell them apart."

"And what are those crooked fences over there?" asked Ellinore, pointing toward the fields of brown stubble ahead.

"Oh, they're worm fences. They keep the animals out of the corn and tobacco. They look like they're falling down because the posts aren't dug in the ground. That way we can move them quickly to another field."

"I imagine your dear mother is buried nearby, isn't she?' Ellinore asked in a quiet voice.

"Yes," said Susannah, "her grave is at the edge of the woods. It's a ways from here beyond the brook and the freshwater spring."

Simon and Spark ran along with them, barking and jumping for attention.

"I didn't expect you'd have dogs here," said Ellinore, bending to scratch Spark between his ears.

"Some settlers bring dogs, but Simon and Spark just wandered by one day and stayed. Papa thinks they once belonged to the Indians."

"Do you feed them?"

"No, they catch their own food in the woods. We wouldn't have enough for them everyday, but sometimes we toss them leftovers. Speaking of food, I expect we should head back and prepare dinner."

When the sun was high, Papa, Jonathan, and Marmaduke came home for dinner, their big meal of the day. The men folk welcomed Ellinore and asked question after question about her voyage while they ate the roasted sweet potatoes with dried beef. Susannah poured a sweet-smelling cider called peach mobby from a cask into a pewter pot. Papa took a swallow first. Then each in turn drank from the same pot.

Ellinore talked and talked. She brought Papa much news from kinfolk in England. Susannah and Jonathan had a new boy cousin, Timothy, born to Papa's brother. And Great Aunt Rebecca Sittwell was doing poorly. Ellinore also talked about everyone on shipboard. "Our captain had been a seaman on the *Ark* and told us about the first English people who came to Maryland nearly thirty years ago on his ship and on the other ship, the *Maryland Dove*."

"Ah, the *Dove*," said Papa with interest.

Susannah smiled. She wasn't sure which her father enjoyed more—learning about history or reciting for others what he already knew—but either way, Susannah knew that stories of long ago took years off his face.

"Did he tell you what happened to the *Dove*?" asked Papa. He put his elbows on the table and leaned forward.

"Indeed, he did," said Ellinore. "When we hit our first huge storm, the captain said it was just a squall. It couldn't be compared to the wind and waves that caused the *Dove* to be lost at sea for a while. He said we had nothing to fear, but I wasn't certain about that. Waves were crashing over the deck, and the wind was fierce. I thought we might well turn over."

"And when the *Ark* stopped first in the West Indies," said Papa, clearly unable to stop himself from continuing the story, "her passengers told the natives that the *Dove* had gone down with everyone lost. But some days later, while the colonists were packing the *Ark* with fresh vegetables and fruits for the rest of their voyage, the *Dove* sailed into the harbor, no worse for the wear. She hadn't sunk after all but had returned to England to wait for better weather to start again."

"That's a grand story," said Ellinore, looking around the table at Papa, Jonathan, Marmaduke, and Susannah.

Even Jonathan managed a half-smile and said, "I hope you fare well here, Ellinore."

Susannah noticed Jonathan's look and was glad that her brother seemed a bit happier.

When Jonathan and Marmaduke had gone outside after dinner, Papa turned to Ellinore. "You'll help Susannah with the corn grinding, washing, milking, cooking, and mending five days a week and Saturday morning. Servants have Saturday afternoon off, and Sunday is a day of rest for all of us. Keep in mind that these first months here are your seasoning time. It's a time to get used to the water, food, and humid weather. Many settlers fall ill. Some don't live long, God rest their souls. And let's hope the mosquitoes don't take a fancy to you. They bring the fever."

"I will be careful," said Ellinore. "I want to touch and smell and see and taste and hear most everything in Maryland! I can't think about taking sick."

"We are thankful that you've arrived safely," said Papa. "At the new year next March, you'll have charge of my twin sons, William and Henry. They're a year old now. I board them across the river with the Halls. I pay Goodman Hall in leaves of tobacco."

"Does he own land here like you do?" asked Ellinore.

"Not yet. He works as a tenant farmer for Mr. Laval. Goodman and Goodwife Hall came here as bonded servants just as my wife and I did."

"You've been fortunate, haven't you, with your crops," said Ellinore. "A middling farmer like you wouldn't have these chances in England."

"That's true," said Papa, nodding his head. "The soil is good. Our crops, especially tobacco, grow well. If only we didn't have to worry about meeting an early death." Papa paused for a moment. "And

Ellinore, you must stay out of the sun as much as possible. Its rays are much hotter here than in England."

When the men went back to work for the afternoon, Ellinore and Susannah cleared the table, swept the hall, and chopped carrots and turnips from their root cellar to add to the evening stew of corn and rabbit.

After they finished, Susannah told Ellinore to rest awhile. "You have to watch over yourself and not get too tired." She arranged her own mattress near the fire and motioned for Ellinore to lie down. "Tonight I'll find bedding for you in our linen chest. Papa says he wants to buy bedsteads when he is paid for this year's tobacco crop. We won't have to sleep on the floor anymore."

Ellinore stepped out of her worn, flat, black shoes and pulled off her cap to let down her matted hair. "I have something packed in my chest to give you. When we go outdoors later, I'll find it. I only hope you don't have one already."

6

A SAD VISITOR

THAT AFTERNOON SUSANNAH HELPED Ellinore open her well-worn trunk. Tiny and not so tiny black insects tumbled out of Ellinore's dirty, wrinkled petticoats, stockings, aprons, and bedroll. Susannah and Ellinore shook everything vigorously.

"We'll wash in the morning," said Susannah. "The sun goes down early in November. Nothing'll dry now."

Susannah stopped to stare at a wooden frame that Ellinore was holding.

"A looking glass!" she cried. "How beautiful."

"It was given to me by my godmother," said Ellinore, handing it to Susannah. "And I'm giving it to you."

"Oh, thank you, Ellinore!" said Susannah. She held the looking glass at arms' length and stared in it. "My eyes are gray, aren't they?"

"With beautiful dark eyelashes, too," said Ellinore.

Susannah looked down, bashful but pleased.

"I'll fasten it by the door," she said, "so we can see ourselves in the light. Now I won't have to beg Papa to buy a looking glass from Mr. Laval's store."

"Cousin Matthew isn't interested in silly things like looking glasses, I suppose," said Ellinore. "We'll see if he glances at himself on his way out the door."

"He might well peer at himself in one," said Susannah, "but he wouldn't spend a leaf of his tobacco to buy one. He'd buy a hog or another cow."

"Your father's thinking of the future, isn't he?" asked Ellinore.

"Yes. He doesn't want Jonathan, the twins, and me to be left poor orphans if he dies." Susannah was silent a moment, then went on. "I can't think of Papa dying. Did you know that Mama lost three children after I was born?"

Ellinore started to answer but stopped to point toward Papa's fallow fields. "Someone's coming this way. An old man."

Susannah stood quickly. "It looks like Asa Orrick the Elder," she cried. "He owns the big plantation next to us. His son is known as Asa the Younger."

"He's having trouble walking," said Ellinore.

"We must go to him. He's been very sick. His wife passed away just before Mama died last spring."

Susannah and Ellinore tossed everything back

into the chest and raced across the fields. Mr. Orrick was out of breath and barely able to stand when they reached him. They grabbed his trembling arms to steady him.

"Mr. Orrick," cried Susannah, "what're you doing way out here in the fields? We'll help you back to your plantation."

"No, no," whispered the old man. "I must speak to your father, Susannah." Mr. Orrick's brown leather doublet and breeches hung in loose folds on his bent figure.

"He's at work in our tobacco drying house. Come, rest at our hearth while I fetch him."

Soon Papa was seated at the table with Mr. Orrick, who seemed stronger as he sipped from the pot of apple cider that Susannah held for him. Ellinore knelt by the hearth and stirred the fish stew with the catch that Marmaduke had brought in that morning.

"Asa, what brings you here?' said Papa. "You shouldn't have ventured this far alone."

"Matthew," said Mr. Orrick, taking a deep breath, "for the first time in all my years as a planter, one of my servants, Benjamin Duckett, has run away. Do you know how long he has been gone?"

"Less than a fortnight," answered Papa. "Jacob Hewett came here to tell us to be on the watch for him."

Susannah noticed Mr. Orrick's face fall and his shoulders slump when he heard this news. Finally he shook his head and spoke in a sorrowful voice. "To think I trusted him. The deception stings."

Susannah looked away guiltily. She busied herself by peering over Ellinore's shoulder.

"I handed over my faith and a fair amount of my purse that he should oversee my servants. Benjamin ran away more than seven days past, and I found out only today."

Susannah's shoulders loosened, realizing it was the overseer and not Benjamin who angered Mr. Orrick.

"How is that so, Asa?" said Papa.

"I've been laid up with this dreadful fever for weeks. Jacob told the other servants that I was too ill to be informed about Benjamin. With my son upriver it was easy for Jacob to deceive me."

"Why would Jacob keep this news from you?"

"Jacob thinks he is in charge of my plantation. When his wife and only son died of the fever and his farm failed some time back, I hired him to give him a new start. He has caused trouble ever since, but he is a hard worker and I need his labor. I have always treated my hired men and servants with fairness."

Papa nodded in agreement. "You have, sir. How did you find out about Benjamin if not from Jacob?"

"I felt stronger this morning and came to the table

for breakfast. I asked my house servant, Mary Catherine, where Benjamin was. At first she wouldn't speak. Finally she told me that Benjamin had escaped."

"Your son, Asa the Younger, should be home to help you," said Papa.

"That is the reason I've come to you, Matthew," said Mr. Orrick. "Ever since this last sickness overtook me, I've asked and asked Jacob to bring my son home. He always promised me, but Young Asa never came. I feared that he was dead." Old Mr. Orrick paused to catch his breath and then went on. "Now I understand. That scoundrel Jacob Hewett never sent anyone upriver to fetch him. While I've been ill and my son away, Jacob doesn't have to answer to anyone."

"I want to help you," said Papa. "What can I do?"

"Would you permit Jonathan and your servant to take your canoe upriver to my outlying fields? Have them tell my son to make haste to my side." Mr. Orrick paused, then added, "I might as well have hired the devil himself to oversee my servants."

"You have my word that Jonathan and Marmaduke will leave early on the morrow," said Papa. "They can hail a ride across the river and borrow Samuel Laval's boat. Ours is missing."

Asa Orrick's tired eyes snapped open. "I suppose Benjamin took it to escape!"

"We know nothing," said Papa. "I must tell you that though the canoe disappeared at the time he ran away, I don't want to think of Benjamin as a thief. He seemed a decent, hardworking lad."

"He was that indeed," agreed Asa Orrick.

Susannah was thankful that Papa hadn't asked her any questions, but she had been quite unsettled this whole visit. Her heart jumped about most when the talk turned to the boat. She wanted so much to believe that Benjamin hadn't taken it.

Finally Mr. Orrick grasped the edge of the table and tried to stand. "At last I know young Asa will come home," he said. "I must not tarry. Thank you kindly for listening to an old man."

"Asa," said Papa, taking hold of Mr. Orrick's arm. "Stay the night here. You're not strong enough to venture home now."

"No, no," said Mr. Orrick with a sigh. "I cannot be away from my land. Jacob Hewett will know I suspect something is wrong."

"Very well," said Papa. "But sit and rest awhile longer. Marmaduke will accompany you home. He's a strong and able man." Papa turned to Susannah and asked her to bring Marmaduke to the house.

Susannah nodded and returned in a few minutes. "Marmaduke's washing at the stream. He'll come soon."

She joined the others at the table and took a drink

from the cider pot. When Marmaduke came in, he and Papa helped the old man to his feet and led him outside. Slowly Mr. Orrick and Marmaduke trudged across the fields with Marmaduke's strong arms keeping Asa the Elder from falling. Spark and Simon raced up from the water and trotted beside them.

As Susannah closed the door she glanced down the wishing path and wondered where Benjamin might be. She had made no wishes today. How could she wish away her own foolishness? It upset her that one promise made in haste could cause such worry.

"Will my chest be safe outside till morning?" asked Ellinore.

Susannah's thoughts were so far away that she stared at Ellinore in surprise.

"Let's bring it in for the night," she finally answered.

After supper Susannah opened the family's wooden chest. "I'll find you a quilt and a pillow, Ellinore, and then you must go right to bed. Your first day in Maryland has been frightfully long."

"I am tired to my bones," said Ellinore, "but still joyous to be here. My head is spinning with questions to ask you."

"Perhaps you can keep them for tomorrow. We can talk while we work."

Susannah glanced about the hall for a spot

where Ellinore might sleep and keep her things. She noticed the twins' empty cradles standing on end in a far corner. A pang of loneliness crept over her as she pulled the cradles near the ladder up to the loft. Marmaduke would take them up to be stored.

"I've made some room for you over here, Ellinore," said Susannah. "We don't have much space, but at least you'll have a corner to call your own."

"My thanks to you!" replied Ellinore. "Your house is like a king's castle after the sleeping quarters on the ship."

After taking off her outer clothes, Ellinore knelt down on her mattress to say her prayers. When Susannah looked over again, she was sound asleep.

Before closing the family chest, Susannah reached to the bottom and pulled out Papa's two prayer books. She held them lovingly, remembering when Papa and Jonathan had taught her to read a little. But that was before Mama took sick. Now there was no time for books.

"I'll fix food for you and Marmaduke to take tomorrow when you go upriver," Susannah told her brother, who was whittling an axe handle by the fire. "There was a red sky tonight. It'll be a good day tomorrow. You should catch a ride quickly to Laval's Landing."

Jonathan nodded but didn't answer. Susannah

knew he was thinking about their lost boat. Mr. Laval's canoe was longer and heavier and harder to paddle.

THE NEXT MORNING Marmaduke reported at breakfast that Mr. Orrick had arrived home safely.

"Will he call the sheriff to look for Benjamin and our boat?" Jonathan asked.

"Mr. Orrick is too ill to do much until his son returns to settle matters."

Susannah's heart stopped when she realized that the sheriff might find Benjamin and bring him—and all his secrets— back.

7

AN UNEXPECTED SUNDAY OUTING

NOVEMBER FROSTED OVER INTO DECEMBER. The winds off the tidewater were brisk and chilly. Tiny ice crystals covered the ground each morning, but the late autumn sun brought a touch of warmth during the day. Papa predicted an open winter with little snow.

Brown Betty had stopped giving milk. She would roam free for the winter with all the other cattle and hogs from nearby plantations. Come spring the planters would claim the animals that were to be sold or slaughtered for food.

Since Ellinore's arrival, Susannah found the days flying by. They worked together on all the chores: cooking ground corn in various ways, salting meat, pressing apples for cider, mending clothes, and making soap and butter. Even the tiresome grinding of corn didn't last so long with Ellinore taking a turn to crush the hard kernels.

Some days Ellinore would talk about her life in England. Today she asked Susannah if she knew about Maryland's early days.

"Oh, yes," said Susannah. "Mama told me about it. The king of England gave all the land around here to a gentleman named George Calvert. He was the first Lord Baltimore. George Calvert wanted to start a colony where people could be free to go to church where they wanted to."

"Is George Calvert living here?"

"Oh, no. He died before he could make the journey. His son Cecil got the land and named it for the king's wife. Her real name was Henrietta Maria, but the king always called her Mary. Cecil never came here either."

"Now I remember," said Ellinore. "The captain told us that Cecil Calvert sent his brother, Leonard, to start the colony."

"And two days after Leonard Calvert landed he bought Maryland from the Yaocomico Indians. He traded axes, hoes, knives, and pieces of cloth for the land. He became the first governor and built a fort and a storehouse in St. Mary's City. Papa will take us there sometime."

"Where are the Indians now?" asked Ellinore.

"Some live upriver. Papa traded tools with them for our log canoe. The Indians built him a good, strong boat. You'll be riding in it if we find it again. There aren't any seats, though. Everyone sits on

53

the bottom of the boat."

"I hope I can have a ride soon," said Ellinore. She paused and asked if the Indians were dangerous.

"I've only seen a few Indians in St. Mary's City where they come to trade. They're friendly. Some speak English. The priests who came on the *Ark* taught them."

"But we're living on their land, aren't we?" said Ellinore.

"Yes. But Papa thinks that some day the Indians will go west and find new places to live."

"That doesn't seem fair to me," said Ellinore.

"I don't know," said Susannah in a quiet voice. She realized that Ellinore often thought about things in ways that had never occurred to her. She wanted to tell her about the wishing path. She also longed to tell her about Benjamin.

THE NEXT SUNDAY afternoon Lewis knocked on the door.

"Mr. Laval has sent me to ferry you and your family across the river to Goodman Hall's house," he told Papa. "My master is saddened that your boat is still gone. He wants you to visit your twin sons."

"Mr. Laval is a kind man," said Papa. "Susannah, Ellinore, and I can take our leave now. Jonathan and Marmaduke will remain here."

The trip over was pleasant and brief. After crossing the river, Lewis tied up the canoe while Papa, Susannah, and Ellinore followed a sandy path to the Halls' place, a tiny house on Mr. Laval's plantation.

Susannah ran ahead when she saw Goodwife Hall step outside to greet the visitors. She was holding Henry, whose red hair caught the sun. Susannah stretched out her arms for the baby and hugged him.

"Welcome!" called Goodwife Hall. "I'm happy to have you come to our humble home. We've heard about your lost boat. What a pity!"

The Halls' four children stood close to their mother. Their oldest daughter, Comfort, carried William.

"Good afternoon," said Papa reaching out for William. "At long last we can visit again."

Susannah, smiling as Henry fiddled with her hair, said, "This is Ellinore. She'll be tending the babies come the new year."

"I'm pleased to make your acquaintance," said Ellinore. "Susannah talks of these handsome little lads all the time."

"And these are our children," said Goodwife Hall proudly. "Comfort is nine years of age. Rachel is seven, Mary Elizabeth is two, and our son Patrick is five."

The three girls smiled shyly and stayed close by their mother's side, but freckled-faced Patrick quickly spoke up. "Are you taking the twins away today?"

"Not today, son," said Papa. "We'll take them

home come spring. Cousin Ellinore just arrived from England to care for them, but she needs time to settle in. We want her to keep her health."

"Oh," said Patrick. "You know, you don't have to take the babies. My mama wants to keep them always!"

"Patrick!" said his mother. "Go into the house. You are not to speak out of turn to Goodman Clark."

Patrick stared at his mother, curled his lower lip, and ran inside.

"It's a good thing his father didn't hear him," said Goodwife Hall, shaking her head. "He'll be back soon. Our woodpile was low. He's gone to split logs. Step inside, won't you please?"

Susannah wondered how Goodwife Hall managed with all these children in her small, cramped house. But no matter how much work she had to do, she never seemed to complain.

Holding Henry over her shoulder, Susannah sat down on the Halls' one long bench, while Comfort poured apple cider into a pot to pass to the guests. Ellinore joined them on the bench. Henry gurgled little secret sounds in Susannah's ear. She loved the feel of him against her chest.

"I'll surely miss these two when they go home!" said Goodwife Hall, throwing a fresh log on the fire. "And will you look at all this red hair!" She looked at Papa. "They're taking right after their father and brother and growing faster than weeds in a tobacco field."

Papa nodded. "They surely have sprouted up lately."

"Yes," agreed Goodwife Hall. "William drinks milk now from a little tin pot that Mistress Laval gave me, but Henry doesn't want to stop nursing yet."

"They look exactly alike," said Ellinore. "How do you tell them apart?"

"Henry chatters all the time," said Goodwife Hall. "William's the quiet one, except when he's hungry. And his eyes are a deeper blue than Henry's."

"I've sorely missed seeing them," said Papa. "I'm grateful to you, Goodwife, for taking them in."

"I'm happy to have them. You see that iron kettle at the hearth. My husband bought it from Mr. Laval's store with the extra tobacco you paid him last month for keeping the twins."

"We could buy our own cow if we had even more tobacco," piped up Patrick.

His mother put her finger to her lips and said sternly, "Hush, Patrick, you're to be seen and not heard. Do you understand?"

"Yes, Ma'am," whispered Patrick with a hurt look.

Ellinore reached for Henry and stood him on the dirt floor. When he took a tiny step, she said, "I think you'll be walking right smartly before long."

To everyone's surprise, Goodman Hall came rushing through the door.

"Good day," he said. "I have just spoken to Tobias Pierce. He brings sad news from the Orrick plantation. Old Asa Orrick passed away in his sleep early this morning."

"God rest his soul," said Goodwife Hall, making the sign of the cross.

"He was one of our finest settlers," said Goodman Hall.

"I never knew him to make a dishonest tobacco trade or borrow anything that he didn't return," said Papa. "And he has passed away without knowing what happened to his servant Benjamin Duckett."

"The funeral will be Tuesday before noon," continued Goodman Hall. "Tobias Pierce wants us to bring as much food as we can for the funeral feast. After Mr. Orrick's will is read, everyone will be repaid."

Susannah was silent on the boat ride home. She felt empty one minute, then full of sad memories of Mama's death and funeral the next. As she, Ellinore, and Papa walked slowly to their house from the water, Susannah tried to make a wish but found she couldn't wish for anything that day. Besides, it occurred to her that she had never wished for anything going up the path toward home. Only away, toward the water.

For all the good it did.

8

TWO STRANGERS

EARLY ON THE MORNING OF ASA THE ELDER'S funeral, Susannah, Papa, Jonathan, Ellinore, and Marmaduke set off across the fields to the Orricks' plantation. They carried two iron kettles of rabbit stew, warm cornbread, a roasted wild turkey wrapped in linen cloths, and a pot of butter. Simon and Spark followed, disappearing now and then to chase a squirrel or a chipmunk.

"I'm hungry already," said Ellinore. "The smell of the cornbread and the turkey is making my mouth water. I never ate turkey in England."

"Wait till you see all the food everyone brings to the funeral feast," said Susannah.

"We'd be there by now if we could have taken our boat," interrupted Jonathan.

"Yes, Son, we would," said Papa, "but there's little wind and the air is mild. We'll arrive well before the funeral begins."

Susannah hated to hear Jonathan complain about their missing canoe. The dreadful possibility that Benjamin had stolen it was never far from her thoughts.

The men strode on ahead of Susannah and Ellinore. Jonathan and Papa carried their fowling pieces over their shoulders.

"Why are there so many fields that don't seem to be used for anything?" asked Ellinore, looking down at the flat, brown land scattered with rotting tree stumps.

"These are Papa's and Mr. Orrick's fallow fields. Most seeds won't grow on the land after three years of tobacco and three of Indian corn have been planted on them. The fields have to stand empty for many years before they can be used again."

"Tobacco is surely an important crop in these parts," said Ellinore, "although we certainly can't eat it."

"Yes," agreed Susannah. "Papa says growing tobacco is the best way to make a living here. People in the Old World want to buy it to smoke in their pipes. In the spring, after this year's crop of leaves has been dried and packed, everyone will help to load the ships at Laval's Landing with wooden casks packed tightly with tobacco."

Susannah and Ellinore hiked on across the fields, stopping once in a while to put down the heavy kettles and rest.

"What's that tumble down house used for, that one over there," asked Ellinore, pointing toward the river. "Surely no one lives there."

"Oh, that's Mr. Orrick's old tobacco drying barn," said Susannah. "His servants built a bigger one on the far side of their fields. They'll burn this one down soon so the nails can be used again."

"I'd like to peek in that barn," said Ellinore. "I don't want to miss anything."

Susannah laughed. "I know you don't, Ellinore, but we'd best get on to the funeral. On our way home, we'll look inside. We'll be leaving before dark."

Neighbors, kinfolk, hired hands, and servants were gathering in the Orrick plantation house when Susannah and Ellinore arrived. A fire blazing on the hearth sent its aroma of pine around the room. As they sat down on wooden crates in the back of the hall, Susannah spotted Jacob Hewett standing near the door.

Susannah looked longingly at Mr. Orrick's carved, wooden chairs with leather seats where the priest, important guests, and family members were seated. "I'd love to sit on a real chair sometime with a back to lean against," she whispered to Ellinore.

Mr. Orrick's body lay in a wooden coffin in front of the hearth. Neighboring women had wrapped his body in winding sheets and spread sprigs of rose-mary, the fragrant herb of remembrance, over him.

Father Larkin, the priest who had buried Mama, led the funeral mass and gave a long sermon. He spoke of Asa Orrick the Elder as a prosperous and honest planter who treated his servants fairly.

During the funeral, Susannah noticed two young men. Although their clothes were no different from the other men, Susannah knew they were strangers. Their hands were far too smooth and clean to be Maryland settlers. Everyone who grew tobacco had rough, brown-stained hands and ragged fingernails. One of the men held a leather-bound book, a bottle of ink, and a quill pen on his lap.

After the funeral, the mourners filed slowly and silently outside to gather around the open, freshly dug grave. Many of the women wept. Mr. Orrick would be buried next to his wife, his grave marked with a small wooden cross.

Before the men closed the coffin and nailed it shut, Susannah glanced inside. Without warning, tears filled her eyes and all the painful, hidden memories of her mother's burial overwhelmed her. She took a deep breath and fumbled in her drawstring bag for a handkerchief to wipe her eyes. Turning to flee into a nearby patch of woods, her knees trembled. As Susannah tried to keep herself from stumbling, she felt a strong arm around her waist. Quietly and steadily, Ellinore led Susannah away from the crowd of mourners. While walking arm-in-arm toward the plantation house, they met the two young men that Susannah had seen seated at the funeral.

"Can we be of service?" one of them asked.

"Oh, no, thank you kindly," said Ellinore. "We've just stepped away from the burial for a moment or two."

"Why don't you sit here," the young man suggested, pulling up a nearby bench. "My name is Peter Hudden, and this is my brother, Garret. We are traveling in North America from the Netherlands."

"Please forgive us if our English is not well-spoken," added Garret. "We usually speak in Dutch."

Ellinore started to introduce Susannah and herself, but her words were erased by the sound of gunshots. The militia men had begun shooting off two pounds of gunpowder in Mr. Orrick's memory. After the noise of the shots died down, Ellinore told the young men her and Susannah's names and asked, "Have you been at the plantation for long?"

"Our guide led us ashore four days ago," said Garret. "When we were in London we chanced to meet a cousin of Asa Orrick the Elder. He gave us a letter to bring to him, but Mr. Orrick was gravely ill when we arrived and passed away before he could read it."

"Where are you traveling from here?" Susannah asked. She felt stronger now that she was away from the burial grounds.

"We're searching for land in Maryland or in Nieuw Netherland. The members of our church in Holland want to settle in America."

"Can you tell us about your book?" asked Susannah. She had never before seen anyone carrying a book, quill, and bottle of ink.

"It is a journal of our travels," explained Peter. He opened the book on his lap.

"Peter draws pictures, too, and makes prints of leaves and flowers," said Garret. "Show them your sketches of the upriver Indians that we recently visited and the woodland animals and trees. We have never been in such thick forests before, and we are amazed to see groves of trees where the sun doesn't shine through."

Susannah and Ellinore stood up so Peter could spread out his journal on the bench. He carefully opened it, revealing drawings of a longhouse, faces of Indians, fish, trees, and a running deer. They had been drawn by a sure, steady hand. Susannah was quite taken with their artistry. As Peter leafed through the pages, Susannah caught sight of a sketch of the head and shoulders of a young man with a slight beard and ears that stuck out. He was wearing a knit cap.

Peter turned the page. Susannah's heart caught in her throat.

"Please, sir," she said slowly, "could you turn back to that picture of the boy, the one who doesn't look like an Indian."

"Susannah must mean that lad we saw at the Indian village," said Garret to his brother. "We thought he might be English, but he wouldn't speak to us."

"Yes," agreed Peter. "He hurried away when I asked him if he spoke English or Dutch. I didn't have a chance to finish his picture. Several Indian boys came by and wanted to pose for me."

When Peter turned back to the picture, Susannah bent down to look more closely. As sure as the sun set in the west, she knew it was Benjamin.

"Why was he with the Indians?" she asked, trying to sound casual.

"We know not," said Peter. "Our Indian guide spoke some English but kept silent when we inquired about him."

Ellinore peered at the picture.

"Do you recognize this boy, Susannah?" asked Ellinore.

"I–I don't know," said Susannah, wondering how much she had given away, wondering how much she should give away. "For a moment I thought I knew him."

"Really?" asked Ellinore. "Who do you think he is?"

Susannah looked at her cousin directly. The words spilled out.

"Benjamin Duckett, Mr. Orrick's runaway servant, the one Jacob Hewett thinks stole our boat."

Before Ellinore could respond, Peter Hudden abruptly closed his journal and tucked it under his arm.

"We must be on our way to pay our respects to Asa Orrick the Younger," said Garret. "Good day." The two men moved quickly toward the burial ground.

"Why did they scamper away from us so hastily?" asked Susannah, in a bewildered tone.

"They seemed alarmed when you said the boy might be a runaway servant," said Ellinore. "They may be afraid someone will ask them questions. They're strangers here and probably don't want to be caught in our affairs."

"Yes," agreed Susannah. "They probably know that it's bad for a servant to run away."

"Do you feel strong enough to join the others now?" asked Ellinore.

"Oh, yes," answered Susannah, glad for a change of topic. "I'm fine now."

"I haven't seen so many people together since the ship," said Ellinore, looking at the crowd walking toward the plantation house.

"Settlers come from all around to a funeral. It's the only time we really gather together. Everyone wants to talk and find out the news. Many of these people came to Mama's funeral."

Susannah and Ellinore helped the neighboring women serve the food and drink. They heard the colonists talk about tobacco prices, the coming winter, and what might be in old Asa Orrick's will.

On one of their trips into the kitchen to refill cider and rum casks, Susannah met Goodwife Hall and Comfort, each carrying a twin.

"I didn't see you at the funeral," said Susannah.

"Heaven forbid!" exclaimed Goodwife Hall. "Henry and William are much too lively to attend a funeral. We just arrived on a boat with some traders from upriver. The other children are somewhere about with their father and Mistress Laval and her family."

"Susannah and I haven't eaten yet. Why don't you take your meal with us?" said Ellinore. "We'll bring as much as we can carry for all of us."

They moved closer to the house and pulled up two empty benches. Soon Susannah and Ellinore returned with wooden platters heaped with all the tasty fare of the funeral feast. While they devoured their food and licked the last morsels from their fingers, Papa and Young Asa joined them. Mr. Orrick's son was dressed in his finest clothes with a sword at his side. Susannah thought he looked grand indeed in his dark wool suit with silver buttons, white shirt, and black beaver hat with a huge, red, curving plume.

"Mr. Orrick," said Goodwife Hall, "how saddened I am about your father's death. May he rest in peace."

"I will miss him greatly," said Asa the Younger. "I fear though that I will have little time to mourn. I must arrange for the reading of Father's will. And I haven't found a new servant yet to replace Benjamin."

Susannah thought of telling Young Asa about the sketch in Peter Hudden's journal, but was it really Benjamin? Perhaps she was mistaken. All of a sudden she realized that if it was his picture, she could also tell Papa about seeing it. And she would never have to explain meeting Benjamin that evening at the river.

For a moment Susannah felt as though a great millstone had been lifted from her shoulders. She would be free of the terrible lie and of her guilty feelings that never seemed to go away. The sheriff's men would find Benjamin with the Indians. Benjamin certainly wouldn't tell anyone that he had seen her the night he left. If he had stolen the canoe, the sheriff would surely find that as well. But still she felt she had done something wrong. And what would happen to Benjamin?

9

A SHOCKING DISCOVERY

AS GOODWIFE HALL AND THE CHILDREN moved on to talk to other settlers, Papa spoke to Susannah. "I want you and Ellinore to start home soon. Darkness falls fast now."

"When are you coming?" asked Susannah.

"Jonathan, Marmaduke, and I will follow shortly. With all the feasting today, we'll need only a small supper when we get home."

After many goodbyes, Susannah and Ellinore gathered their kettles and turned homeward. Simon and Spark, who had been snatching leftovers all day, appeared at their heels, ready to dash off across the fields.

"Did you tell your father about the picture?" Ellinore asked.

"No, I didn't!" Susannah answered sharply. She paused and realized how she must have sounded. "Oh, Ellinore, I've spoken crossly. Forgive me."

"Do not fret," said Ellinore gently. "Today has been a painful time for you."

"We can look in the old tobacco house on our way home," said Susannah more cheerfully. "I know you're curious to see if there's anything inside other than old leftover tobacco leaves."

"Oh, it's probably just filled with cobwebs and bats, but if there's time, I'd like to peek in quickly," said Ellinore.

They hiked at a good pace to the weather-beaten barn and put down their kettles.

"Goodness," exclaimed Ellinore, "what a heavy board bars the door."

Susannah and Ellinore pushed the board loose from its support and yanked open the creaking door. They paused on the threshold to adjust their eyes to the dim light and stepped inside.

Suddenly Susannah dug her fingers into Ellinore's arm.

"Our boat! Look, here's Papa's mark!" She traced the letters "M. C." carved on the bow of the boat that filled much of the old tobacco house. "Who do you suppose . . . ?"

A harsh voice interrupted her. "You are trespassing on private property! Be off, both of you. The sheriff will hear of this soon enough."

Susannah and Ellinore whirled around to find themselves face to face with Jacob Hewett.

Scared half to death by Hewett's sudden, menacing appearance, Susannah's anger nevertheless far outweighed her fear. "Why is my father's boat in here?" she asked accusingly. "It's been missing for weeks!"

"You heard me," snarled Jacob Hewett, ignoring her question. "Be off with you!" He strode over to the two and rudely pushed them out the door.

Acting quickly on instinct, and without a word, Susannah shoved the door shut, trapping Jacob Hewett inside the old barn. She held the latch tightly, while Ellinore swiftly replaced the board across the door. They could hear Jacob Hewett banging and shouting as they tore away toward the plantation house, their kettles forgotten.

"We must find Papa," cried Susannah breathlessly. She turned to the dogs who were yelping about her feet. "Go, Simon and Spark. Find Papa now!"

"I hope Jacob Hewett doesn't escape," said Ellinore.

They came upon Goodwife Hall and the children heading toward the river with Tobias Pierce, who would ferry them home.

"Goodwife Hall, have your seen my father?" asked Susannah with a hurried voice.

"The last I saw of him, he was with Asa the Younger, walking toward the new tobacco barn. Whatever is the matter, child?"

Susannah and Ellinore ran on without answering.

"I'll look in the house and other buildings around here," said Ellinore. "You go straight to the barn. We mustn't waste time. Jacob Hewett might be able to break down the door from the inside."

Susannah nodded and disappeared into a stand of thick evergreens. Feeling hot and dusty all over, Susannah wondered if she would ever again catch her breath. She crossed a broad field of tobacco stubble and followed the dogs toward the new barn. They were already jumping on Papa and Young Asa when Susannah arrived.

"Papa!" called Susannah. "We found our boat! Ellinore and I. It's in that old tobacco barn. The one by the water. We shut Jacob Hewett inside! He stole it! I know he did! Come now before he gets away!"

"My child," said Papa, "have you no respect for the dead, shouting so loudly?" He put his hand on her shoulder. "Tell me in a quiet voice what has happened. Are you certain it is our boat?"

"Oh, yes, Papa. It is our boat. I saw your letters, M. C., on the bow. I know I did."

"Matthew, we have no time to talk," interrupted Asa the Younger. "You go directly to the barn. I'll summon my servants and follow in haste."

"Come, Papa, now!" said Susannah, pulling his arm.

"Jacob Hewett's always had a mean spirit, but I

never thought him a thief." said Papa. "Find Jonathan."

As Ellinore caught up with them, Susannah motioned for her to turn back and follow Papa. The news about Jacob Hewett spread quickly among the settlers at the funeral. Soon a crowd gathered around the door of the old barn.

"I hear him banging," said Papa.

"Stand away," shouted Young Asa, as he lifted the board from the door. Jacob Hewett leaped out, his dark face twisted in anger and contempt.

"I'll have the sheriff . . ." Jacob abruptly stopped talking when he saw Young Asa facing him. Jonathan and Marmaduke pinned his arms behind him.

"Jacob, you have betrayed my father's trust," said Young Asa. "First, one of our servants ran away, and you kept the news from him. Now it seems you have hidden Goodman Clark's canoe. The sheriff is upriver. When he returns I will report your wrongdoings to him. Until then you will remain under guard in the servants' quarters."

"I am innocent of any wrongdoing," roared Jacob Hewett. Marmaduke and Jonathan strengthened their grip on him, while everyone else stared in silence and disbelief.

"Asa," said Papa coming out of the tobacco house, "there are many barrels of tobacco behind my boat."

Young Asa shook his head in dismay. "My father

and I *thought* some tobacco was missing. Jacob Hewett's crimes grow longer and longer."

Young Asa beckoned to two of his servants who were striding toward the barn. "Take this common thief away. Tie him up and do not take your eyes off him until I return."

"I still can't believe our boat's back," said Susannah. She looked up at Papa and Young Asa, her gray eyes dancing. "I was afraid it was gone forever."

"Our governor should be proud of you and Ellinore," said Young Asa. "Imagine two young ladies catching a thief!"

Jonathan looked at the boat, shaking his head, then at his sister. A broad smile broke over his narrow face. She nearly laughed with the joy of it.

"Why do you suppose Jacob Hewett stole our boat?" Papa asked Young Asa. "And how did he get it?"

"I suspect he took it while searching for Benjamin on the night he ran away," said Young Asa. "Jacob knew that I had our boat upriver. He saw a chance to hide yours until he needed it, and blame it on Benjamin. Jacob probably planned to carry his stolen tobacco in it to a trading ship bound for Europe."

"Didn't he think he would be caught? My mark's carved on the bow," said Papa, shaking his head.

"I suspect he wouldn't move the tobacco till

spring and by then he would have worked out some scheme to try to fool us," replied Asa. "When Jacob's wife died and he fell on hard times some years back, my father offered to pay his passage back to England.

"What will happen to him now?" asked Jonathan.

"The judge at St. Mary's City will certainly order him to work off his debts to me and to your father," said Asa. "T'would be foolish to lock up a strong man when we need his labor."

"Won't he cause more trouble?" asked Jonathan.

"I think not," said Young Asa. "Jacob knows my father left him some livestock in his will. He won't get it if he causes more trouble. Tobias Pierce and I will keep our hawk eyes on him. One bad move and Jacob Hewett will be worse off than a cow stuck in the spring mud."

Jonathan seemed satisfied with this answer. He looked at Susannah again, and she saw in his eyes relief, weariness, and respect.

"Papa," said Jonathan, "Marmaduke and I will take the boat home now."

"Stay near shore," said Papa. "We'll help you load up our belongings."

"Cousin Matthew," said Ellinore, "would you allow me to go home in the boat too? I'll help paddle."

"Paddling a heavy log canoe's hard work, but you may go, Ellinore," answered Papa.

"Ever since I came to these shores your boat's been gone. I would very much like a ride. I promise not to tip it over!"

Susannah and Papa waved to the others and started for home across the darkening fields. Simon and Spark seemed to come out of nowhere to follow them.

As they parted, Ellinore called, "Susannah, don't forget to tell your father about the drawing that might be Benjamin Duckett."

10

ON THE WAY HOME

"BENJAMIN DUCKETT?" ASKED PAPA. "IS THERE news of him?"

"Ellinore and I saw a drawing today of a young man who might be Benjamin." As Susannah spoke she felt her new feelings of happiness draining away.

"A drawing?" asked Papa. "Whatever do you mean?"

"Did you meet the two travelers from across the seas who came to the funeral? They are brothers, Peter and Garret Hudden."

"No, I didn't speak to them, but I heard they are looking for land."

"Peter showed us his book. A *journal* he called it. He writes about their travels and draws pictures with a quill. He had sketches of the upriver Indians and their animals. As he turned the pages of the journal, I saw a sketch of a white boy wearing a knit cap. I thought he looked like Benjamin Duckett."

"It is possible that Benjamin went to work for the Indians when he ran away. No one has brought back any word about him from the northern colonies." Papa stared at Susannah for a moment. "Did you tell Asa the Younger about the picture?"

"No, Papa," mumbled Susannah, feeling ashamed.

"You should have come to me immediately. Young Asa must be told on the morrow. Marmaduke will have to take a message to him at daybreak. The brothers may be traveling onward very soon. Young Asa will want to see the picture."

"I don't think they will show it to him," said Susannah. "They turned away when Ellinore asked if Benjamin was the runaway servant."

"They don't understand how valuable servants are here. That's all the more reason why you should have told Young Asa. He sorely needs strong workers."

Susannah was silent for a moment and then in a whisper said, "Papa, there's something else about Benjamin . . ." She swallowed hard, and rushed on. "I didn't tell you the truth that night I was late, late coming from the river. Do you remember? The dogs found Benjamin in the woods. He was running away that night. I talked to him. I made a promise to him that I wouldn't tell anyone."

Papa stopped short. "Susannah, why would you make such a promise?"

"I felt bad for Benjamin. He said Jacob Hewett mistreated him and didn't always give him enough to eat. Benjamin didn't know how to fight back. I wanted to help him get away. I didn't think about anything else that might happen."

Papa looked at her in disbelief. "Benjamin broke the Maryland law when he escaped. He made a bond with Old Asa Orrick to work for him until he had paid back his ship passage from England."

Tears filled Susannah's eyes. "I told Benjamin to go to county court, but he said he wasn't free. He thought no one would listen to him."

"He was a foolish lad to give up without trying. And you were even more foolish to make a promise to him that would keep the truth from all of us."

Susannah was silent for a moment. "I know I made a serious mistake, Papa."

"Yes, you did. If you had told me when you first saw Benjamin, the men would probably have brought him back quickly. The judge would have heard his story, and Asa the Younger would have dealt with Jacob Hewett for mistreating a servant."

"I understand," murmured Susannah, and then added in a brighter voice, "but it was good fortune that Ellinore and I found our boat today, wasn't it, Papa?"

"It was, indeed," said Papa, with a smile that seemed to play on his face without his consent.

Susannah hoped he would say something more, but they walked on in the moonlight for a long while without another word. The only sounds were the crunching of their feet on the dry grass, the distant hooting of owls, and the scurrying of small animals.

When they were nearly home, Susannah asked, "Do you think Young Asa will send someone upriver to look for Benjamin?"

"As soon as he hears that Benjamin may be with the Indians he'll dispatch Tobias Pierce to find him and bring him back. Young Asa believed that Benjamin had followed the creeks up north in our boat and would stow away on a ship back to England."

"Papa," continued Susannah in a quiet voice, "are you going to tell Asa the Younger that I knew about Benjamin?"

"There is no need," answered Papa gently, "but you must reckon with Jonathan, and yourself, of course."

"I will. Jonathan may be very angry at me, but that will be my due." She paused, then asked, "If Benjamin is brought back, will he be whipped with many lashes because he ran away?"

"I don't think the judge would sentence a young man like Benjamin to such a cruel punishment. He will, though, have to work longer to make up his lost time before he is granted his freedom."

"Won't Jacob Hewett try to mistreat him again?"

"Asa the Younger would never allow a servant of his to be harmed. I don't think Benjamin has anything to fear from Jacob Hewett now."

Susannah nodded, and both father and daughter fell silent for the rest of the way home.

"Come, have corn porridge with us," called Ellinore when Papa and Susannah arrived at the door. "You must be hungry by now, though we surely filled our bellies at the funeral feast. We had a glorious boat ride home too!"

"The canoe didn't tip at all," said Marmaduke with a laugh. "Ellinore's a worthy sailor."

Susannah pretended to eat but quickly left the table to sit by the hearth. She knew she should help Ellinore clean up and set the night fire, but she couldn't find the strength to stand up. No one seemed to notice her except Spark and Simon, who nuzzled close. As she scratched their ears her eyes closed, and her head dropped forward in sleep. When she felt Ellinore's hands on her shoulders, Susannah woke with a start.

"Susannah," whispered Ellinore, "come to bed. You've had a long, long day."

A FEW MORNINGS LATER after the men had left for work, Susannah told Ellinore she would gather the day's kindling sticks.

"Don't tarry," said Ellinore, "I promised your father hot cornbread for dinner today."

"And that means extra grinding, of course," answered Susannah. "I'll hurry back." She tied her woolen shawl tightly about her shoulders and picked up a canvas sling to hold the sticks.

Alone at last, except for the company of Simon and Spark, Susannah collected her scattered thoughts of all that had taken place on the day of Mr. Orrick's funeral. The next morning she had followed Jonathan out the door and told him about her promise to Benjamin. He seemed more hurt than angry, and walked away in silence. But at dinner that noon, he had unexpectedly helped her add the heavy logs to the fire. She could tell he had forgiven her. Perhaps he thought she'd done the right thing, after all.

As she ran toward the river, Susannah heard someone calling her name.

"Susannah, Susannah!"

Startled, she stopped and looked about her. Who was calling her? Was she daydreaming? She heard her name again. The voice came from the river.

Three people were waving to her from a passing boat. Susannah dropped her twigs and branches and tore to the water's edge. She recognized Benjamin Duckett paddling a log canoe. With him were Tobias Pierce and one of Asa the Younger's other servants.

"I'm going back to work off my debt," shouted Benjamin. "When I'm allowed free time some Sunday, I'll come visit. I have many things to tell you!"

"Yes, yes, please come soon! Don't forget!" Susannah waved and waved long after his silhouette— overlarge ears and all—had dipped around the bend and disappeared.

Susannah's heart pounded as she collected her kindling sticks. When her sling was full, she knelt down to stroke the dogs.

"Oh, Simon and Spark. I don't think I'll need to make wishes anymore on our path. Many of my wishes have come true, but it was foolish to wish Mama alive again, wasn't it? She is alive inside me all the time. And I'll see Benjamin again. I know I will! I think I missed him."

Susannah Clark smiled to herself and hurried back to the house. Ellinore would be waiting for her to help with the grinding of the day's corn.

HISTORICAL POSTSCRIPT

Most of the first white settlers who came to Maryland from Europe before 1700 arrived as unmarried servants. Free settlers paid for the servants' travel across the Atlantic. The servants then worked off the cost of ship passage with years of service. Some servants, known as indentured servants, came with a written contract. The contracts had indentures (cuts) placed on them for identification. Servants who didn't have this paperwork were known as bonded servants. Their status was essentially the same as that of indentured servants. Most bonded and indentured servants served terms of four or five years. After this period of service they could work for themselves as free men or women. However, children under sixteen years of age, such as the fictional Benjamin Duckett, worked for longer terms, depending upon how young they were.

There was a great shortage of women among 17th-century immigrants, whether they arrived free or as servants. Therefore most men had to wait to marry, if they could marry at all. An ex-servant man usually had to start as a laborer for someone else.

He looked for a wife after he had acquired some property—livestock, for example—and had leased or even purchased some land. An ex-servant woman found a husband quickly. Susannah's mother had not waited long.

Life was not easy for 17th-century settlers. They had to clear the land, build houses and barns, and produce food. The tobacco they grew was sent to Europe in return for manufactured goods. Quite apart from all this work, every immigrant, whether servant or free, faced a first year of "seasoning," a time when their bodies adjusted—or didn't—to their new environment. Diseases such as influenza, dysentery, and typhoid existed in England, but here they came in new strains. Malaria, an intermittent sickness not known in most parts of England, was widespread. Although malaria was not in itself a major killer, it lasted a lifetime and weakened people, allowing them to fall prey to other, fatal diseases. Many servants died before they became free. Nearly all immigrants died sooner than they would have had they stayed in England. The great majority of children lost at least one parent before reaching maturity, and many lost both. In the 1660s, Susannah had so far been lucky. Her father was still alive.

Slowly, life and life expectancies improved. The children born of immigrants and the children they in turn produced were less likely than newcomers to die before their offspring had come of age. Those who survived infancy—and about half did not—developed immunities in childhood to the diseases that had killed their parents or grandparents. Susannah would probably live longer and have more children than her parents had, and likely would survive to become a grandmother. Since children of the native-born had about even sex ratios, over time the shortage of women began to disappear. By the end of the 17th-century the native-born were a majority of the Maryland population. Their longer lives created stronger, more stable families and communities than those of their immigrant ancestors. Unfortunately, stability and health do not necessarily equal wealth. As time went on, the poor had fewer opportunities to acquire land of their own.

By 1700, large landowners were discovering that importing black slaves from Africa was a "better" option than using white indentured servants. White servants became free men and women again at the end of their service, thus requiring replacements. Black people, however, remained slaves for the rest of their lives, never able to buy their own land. Their children, grandchildren, and great-grandchildren were also born into bondage. It wasn't until the American Civil War (1861–1865) that all black people in the United States finally became free citizens. But generations of forced servitude left a deep, lasting scar. All these years later, their descendants—and our nation as a whole—still struggle with the aftermath of slavery.

What of the first inhabitants of the land? There are a few Native Americans still living on their original land in southern Maryland, but early on most disappeared from the area, moving west or dying from diseases spread by the colonists.

By 1700, Susannah Clark's Maryland was beginning to disappear. By the time of the Civil War, with the advent of industry, rail travel, and financial and cultural institutions, Susannah's world was long gone.

DOUBLET – A man's jacket, often without sleeves

MARCH 25 – The first day of the New Year in the Old Style Calendar which the English people used until 1752, when they changed to the calendar in use today

MORTAR – A heavy container used for grinding grain

PESTLE – A metal or wooden tool used to pound or grind grain in a mortar

PEWTER – An alloy or mixture of metals containing tin. The settlers used pewter for household utensils.

SALLET – Salad

WORM FENCE – A type of split-rail fence which the Maryland settlers used to keep cattle and horses out of tobacco and corn fields. The rails were placed in a zigzag pattern without digging posts into the ground. In this way the fence could easily be moved to new fields, but was often blown down by the wind.

NAMES FOR ADDRESSING PEOPLE IN EARLY MARYLAND

GOODMAN – Used when speaking to a small planter such as Susannah's father and Francis Hall, who was a free man but owned no land. A wife would be called GOODWIFE. (A bonded servant such as Benjamin or Ellinore would be called by his or her first name only.)

LORD – Used when speaking to a man of noble birth such as Lord Baltimore. His wife would be called LADY.

MISTER (MR.) – Used when speaking to a large plantation owner such as Asa Orrick. A wife would be called MISTRESS.

YEOMAN – A man who owns a small farm